TAMMY THE TROLL
A DANCE
IN THE FOREST

ONCE UPON A
Dance

Dedicated to
Dance Teachers

DINA MCDERMOTT & ONCE UPON A DANCE
ILLUSTRATED BY CRISTIAN GHEORGHITA

Tammy the Troll
A Dance in the Forest
A Prop-Based Dance Story for Classroom and Anytime Fun

©2023 **Once Upon a Dance** | Redmond, WA
Story by Dina McDermott, www.dinamcdermott.com
Illustrated by Cristian Gheorghita
Photos in Collaboration with Dan Lao Photography
Design in Collaboration with Becky's Graphic Design, LLC

Library of Congress Control Number: 2023908291

Hardcover ISBN: 978-1-955555-66-1
Softcover ISBN: 978-1-955555-65-4
eBook ISBN: 978-1-955555-64-7

Juvenile Fiction: Interactive Adventures; Imagination & Play; Performing Arts: Dance

First Edition

Dear Parents and Teachers,

Tammy the Troll is a story dance I've developed and shared during thirty years as a dance teacher. I hope you and your children/students enjoy this perennial student favorite.

I realize now that this story of a shy misfit breaking out of her shell through the gift of friendship reflects my own journey. I was painfully shy as a child, but dance allowed me to express myself. I've been a dancer all my life, as well as a choreographer, teacher, co-artistic director, dance writer, and community activist.

Please note there are story-leader instructions next to the *handprints*. You can follow these suggestions or use your imagination to make up your own! Set up is easy: tie a scarf to a ballet barre or chair across the room, and get a scarf for each child. This story can be for one student or an entire class. Everyone can do all the movements, or there could be one Tammy and many children.

—**Dina McDermott**, *author*

Enjoy!
Dina McDermott

Hello Fellow Dancers!

Welcome to the story of Tammy the Troll.
I hope you will dance along with Tammy and me.

Two small scarves can make the story even more fun. One could
be your backpack and the other scarf can show where Tammy
lives. You could also just use your imagination—the most important
thing is to enjoy yourself.

Be safe, and do what works for your body in your space.

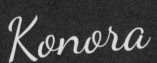

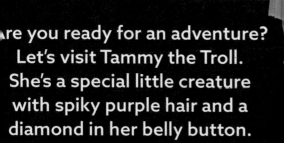

re you ready for an adventure? Let's visit Tammy the Troll. She's a special little creature with spiky purple hair and a diamond in her belly button.

👋 Touch hair and belly.

Tammy lives far, far away in a hollowed-out tree at the edge of the forest.

👋 Point to the other side of the room—where a scarf is tied if using one.

Let's get ready to go. First, get your backpack and put it on your back.

✋ Give each child a scarf.

✋ Demonstrate/help kids tuck scarves into the back tops of leotards or shirts.

We'll leave it there as we pack our supplies. And we'll keep our backpacks on our backs until we need them.

What should we pack?
I know. Let's bring a snack,
a water bottle, a rope, a
flashlight, and a towel.

Have kids volunteer items, too, if there's time.

Put everything in your backpack.
And most importantly, here's a
friendship present for Tammy!

Reach behind and pretend to put
each item into the backpack.

Hold up the present before reaching up and back.

Let's pretend to put on our hiking boots.
✋ Lean forward and tie shoes.

Okay, here we go!
Do you have your walking stick?
✋ Reach out and grab an imaginary stick.

Let's open
the front door
of our house.
Creeeeaakk.
✋ Push the door open.

Stay close and stick together so we don't get lost in the forest.

🖐 March holding the stick.

The trail isn't very far. But, yikes! We have to get through some sticky spider webs.

🖐 Brush cobwebs away and duck low.

Uh oh, the tangled roots are
so high they're blocking our path.

We'll have to step carefully and move slowly so we don't trip.

🖐 Lift knees high to step over the roots.

Oh my! Now there's a tall mountain in our way.

👋 Point to the mountaintop.

Let's use our rope to climb.

👋 Throw a rope over the mountain and climb arm over arm and legs scrambling.

Wow! We're at the top. I can see the whole wide world from up here.

👋 Raise your hand above your eyes and look in every direction.

There's our house...
🖐 Point at the starting place.

...the forest, and Tammy's house.
🖐 Point to the scarf/other

**Let's roll down
the other side of
the mountain.**
🖐 Spin upright or on the
ground with arms at sides

**Whew!
We made it.
Let's wipe off the dirt.**
🖐 Brush arms and torso, lean
forward to brush legs and feet

Here we go.	Here's Tammy's tree house. Let's see if she's home. *Knock, knock*.	The door is slightly open. Let's peek inside.	Hello? Hello? Is anyone home? Where's Tammy?
✋ March.	✋ Knock on an imaginary front door.	✋ Lean sideways to look in.	✋ Lift palms and shrug shoulders.

Let's go downstairs and explore the roots.
👋 Walk while lowering into a crouch.

It's dark down here. Let's use our flashlight. **Look, look, look.**
👋 Turn on flashlight. Aim it around.

Uh oh, mice! And spiders!
👋 Wiggle mice face and paws.

I hope the spiders don't crawl over here.
👋 Crawl on all fours.

**But no Tammy. _Hmm_.
Let's go back upstairs.**

✋ Start walking from a
crouch and get taller.

**Maybe she's up at
the top of the tree.**

✋ Point up, then march upstairs
or climb up a tree, lifting your
opposite arms and legs.

Let's walk out on the branch and look around. Careful! Out we go to the end of the branch.
🖐 Tiptoe, arms out to the side for balance.

Can you see Tammy? There's not enough room to turn around. Let's walk backward. Go slowly.
🖐 Look out with your hand above your eyes. Walk backward.

The branch is thicker now. Let's jump and spin to turn around.
🖐 Jump around with a half-turn.

Hello, Tammy. Hello.
Hello, Tammy. Hello.
I want to be your friend.
Come out and
say hello.

Let's climb
own and wait on
the front porch.
Creeeeaakk.
✋ Climb or march.
Open the door.

A friendship dance might get
Tammy to come out. Hands on
hips. Heel, toe, and feet together.
✋ Extend one leg forward, tap the heel, tap a pointed
toe, then step the feet together. Alternate legs and
repeat three times while singing the *Hello Song*.

Still no
Tammy.
Where is
that silly troll?
✋ Shrug shoulders.

Hmmm.
Let's check out in the forest.

There are so many beautiful trees. Which one is your favorite? Do you like the tall ones that reach up into the sky...

✋ Make a tall shape.

...or the ones shaking hands with their tree friends?

✋ Reach arms sideways and move them up and down.

Oh look!
A bridge.

✋ Point.

Let's slide across.

✋ Sashay (chassé) or
shuffle sideways.

We made it. Be careful
getting off. It's a big step.

✋ Reach a leg out as if
stepping over something.

**Whoa, look!
Who could it be?**
✋ Reach arms out, palms up.

**Purple hair and
a diamond in
her belly button!**
✋ Touch hair and belly.

**It's
Tammy!
Yay!**

"Well, how do you do, Tammy?"

I almost forgot! We have

What's inside?
✋ Open the box lid.

Ah! It's a huge cloud of

...butterflies!

Follow the butterflies over the trees, over Tammy's house, and through the forest.

🖐 Use your scarf as butterfly wings and fly.

The butterflies are tired.
They can fly back into the box and rest.

✋ Hold box and put on the lid.

✋ Help dancers wear or tuck scarves into
a pocket, waistband, or side of a leotard.

Let's invite
Tammy back
to our house.

✋ Point *home*. Hold hands
and march in that direction.

Hmm, we got a little lost
following those butterflies.
This isn't the way we came!

👋 Tap chin and look thoughtful.

What's this?

👋 Gasp.

There's a river in our way!

We're going to have to go down the river to get home. Whoa! Look, someone left a canoe. That's very nice!

✋ Pull the heavy canoe into the river.

Be careful, it's hard to balance.

✋ Lean forward as if holding on. Lift knees and take a big, slow step into the canoe.

Tammy can sit behind us.

✋ Reach a hand to help Tammy.

Don't forget to put on your life jacket.

✋ Zip up the life jacket.

Let's go!

🖐 Use the scarf to paddle—
one hand on either end.

Uh oh, the river is bumpy—there are lots of currents and waves.

🖐 Wiggle and jostle together
in the bumpy canoe.

Uh oh, uh oh! OH NOOOO!

🖐 Gasp!

There's a waterfall ahead!

Hold on!

Aaaaaaaaah!

🖐 Lean back.

🖐 Fall onto the ground.

🖐 Rock back and forth or roll toward a corner of the room so there's more space for the journey *home*.

Okay, let's paddle to
the edge of the river.

✋ Paddle toward *home*
using the scarf.

Get out of the canoe carefully.
We don't want to tip it over.

✋ Lean forward and climb out one foot at a time.

Help kids tuck scarves into a pocket, waistband, or side of a leotard.

Let's help Tammy get out.

Reach a hand and guide Tammy.

Let's tie up the canoe on this branch.

Tie rope to a tree branch.

We need to go back
through the forest to take
Tammy to our house.

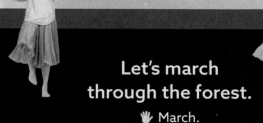

Let's march
through the forest.

✋ March.

Go up over the mountain...

✋ Climb.

...and down the
mountain.

✋ Spin.

Through
the roots.

✋ High step.

Duck under
the spider webs.

✋ Lean and duck.

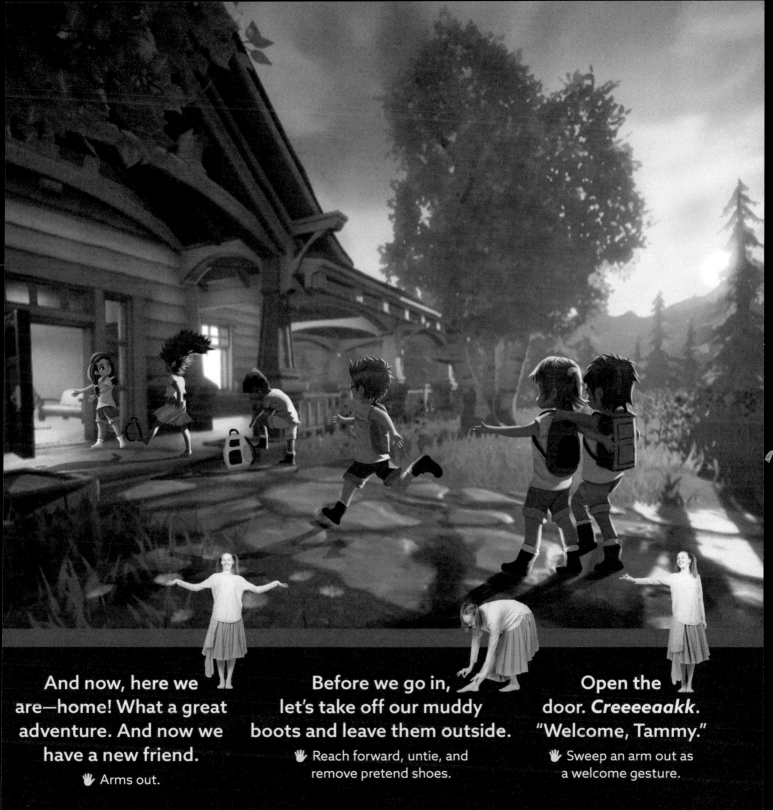

And now, here we are—home! What a great adventure. And now we have a new friend.
👋 Arms out.

Before we go in, let's take off our muddy boots and leave them outside.
👋 Reach forward, untie, and remove pretend shoes.

Open the door. *Creeeeaakk*. "Welcome, Tammy."
👋 Sweep an arm out as a welcome gesture.

I am so happy to have a new friend.
I felt very shy at first,
but I'm not shy anymore.
"Could I give you a hug, Tammy?"

👋 Give a shoulder side hug or cross arms in a hug.

But, oh my. I'm feeling tired
after that adventure. Let's take a nap.
Do you have your pillow? *Aaaa*.

👋 Stretch with a yawn. Use the scarf as a pillow.

Happy sleeping.

👋 Be sure to snore.

Thee End.
The End.

(We end our stories this way in honor of my silly grandpa.)

Thanks for being my dance partner.

I hope you enjoyed the story and will dance with me again sometime.

Until our next adventure,

Love, *Konora*

OPTIONAL DISCUSSION/EXTENSION

Direction:
Review the concept and ask students if they can remember related actions for forward (on the tree branch, through the forest), backward (on the tree branch), up (the tree, the mountain), down (the mountain, the tree, the waterfall), and sideways (chassé/slide across the bridge). Have kids identify traveling movements (going across the bridge) versus in-place actions (tree shapes).

Movement dance/ballet stories:
Discuss other examples students may have seen. Ask them for examples (Swan Lake, Sleeping Beauty, Beauty and the Beast, Snow White, etc.).

Emotions:
Take a moment to discuss stepping out of your comfort zone. Remind kids that it's normal to feel shy meeting new people or nervous trying new things for the first time.

If you repeat the story or use it with older kids, make it more challenging.

- Turned-out (feet and knees facing sideways) marches and/or friendship dance.

- Create a more complicated friendship dance, such as touch toe back, heel tap side, stomp, and three claps. You could even add a spin.

- Add choreography to the butterfly dance or river ride.

- Practice bridge pose (hands and feet on the floor with belly lifted) for the bridge.

- Balance on bottoms, or run and fall down, as you go over the waterfall.

- Use kids' ideas. Play lullaby music and ask them what they think Tammy is dreaming about, or let them make up friendship dances.

DANCE-ALONG STORIES

AGES 4+

AGES 5+

AGES 6+

OTHER SERIES BY ONCE UPON A DANCE

AGES 6+

AGES 8+

Made in the USA
Middletown, DE
10 September 2023

37806777R00022